A KING FOR AMERICA

Secret Discs of a Royal Headhunter

by James Baar

This is a work of political fiction. Any resemblance to persons living or dead is purely coincidental.

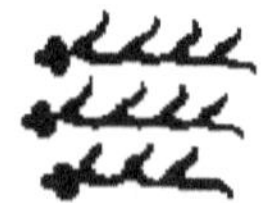

Omegacom

Other Books by James Baar

<u>Fiction</u>

Conversations at the Redwood: The Portraits Speak

The Real Thing and Other Tales

Ultimate Severance

The Great Free Enterprise Gambit

<u>Non-Fiction</u>

Trump Card: Holding America's Enemies at Bay [coauthor William Howard]

Spinspeak II: The Dictionary of Language Pollution

But Wait! There's More! (maybe) [coauthor: Donald E. Creamer]

Combat Missileman [coauthor William Howard]

Table of Contents

A King for America

ROYAL AMERICAN HISTORICAL SOCIETY LIBRARY

My name is George Beowulf Hume and I have agreed willingly -- and probably unwisely -- to record my role in the events that led to the establishment of the United Kingdom of America.

My understanding is that this recorded statement will be impounded in the archives of the Royal American Historical Society Library at the Summer Palace in Newport. Further, I understand that the discs will not be made available to historians and the prurient for at least 100 years. Frankly, I don't believe it. I fully expect before my few remaining years are over to see it all as the basis of some tawdry and sensationalized six-part TV documentary produced through the generosity of some great corporation that really cares. But I will take the chance. My father, who was a professor of history under the old Republic, always told his classes that if the bit players in great events had freely spilled their guts for posterity, history would be a lot livelier subject -- and a lot more instructive. So be it.

As I said, my father Professor Rutherford Ethelred Hume was an historian. He taught for many years at Bowdoin College in Maine. Bowdoin today, of course, is totally French and part of the Institute des Études des Sciences Sociale de Quebec. But at that time it was a small, excellent English-language men's college in what the Guide Michelin now calls le petite ville de Brunswick (two stars for the museum). Brunswick is where I grew up and other than some boyhood nastiness over my cousin Cindy and my early interest in smart phone photography, I can recall no deep childhood traumas that might underlie my professional career. Early on, I did have what some psychologists might call a drive for power. But I never was truly suited for it. I have been told that I have a warm friendly face and manner that inspires confidence -- certainly attributes helpful in achieving high office or selling dubious products. However, I am only five feet tall and, because of my passion for the highly sedentary game of contract bridge and an equal passion for haute cuisine, I have not weighed less than 170 pounds since the age of 19. I have always told my clients in what some kiddingly call the people-packaging biz that, Napoleon aside, in politics a tall, well-proportioned mental zero invariably has the edge.

People packaging, head hunting, has been my life's work. Prior to my first retirement to Sarasota -- now Ciudad de Hernandez -- I was generally regarded in business circles as the leading executive recruiter in the world. There was hardly a major multi-national corporation for which my firm had not provided one or more top executives. Besides our portfolio of blue chips, our client list included such names as the World Bank, the Vatican, Saudi Arabia, and the CIA. An article that, as I recall, appeared in *Forbes once* quoted an anonymous client as saying that on the basis of an 11th hour call we could have filled in a chair at the Last Supper. But I think the editor made that up.

We had our failures, naturally. You can't always open with 100 honors -- a flaw in the natural order that my wife and great bridge partner-for-life, Lillian, finds very irritating. Everyone certainly remembers poor old Roscoe Hunt at Worldwide Food, for example   Terrible as it may seem to say, it was probably just as well that during a security analyst plant tour Roscoe slipped and fell into one of the big vats of Aunt Ida's Down Home Split Pea Soup. As the investigations showed -- and the shareholder suits confirmed -- Roscoe had been really dipping into things long before he fell into the split pea. To cite another example, I certainly share the full blame for Orrin Boon and all of his truly imaginative bookkeeping at International Coagulants that so angered shareholders. Although I must say nothing, he ever did give the lie to my   claim when I placed him there that he was one of the most creative finance managers in the country. If anyone could keep the Titanic afloat, it was Or Boon.

And, speaking of finance managers, who can ever forget Larry Calhoun at Comanche Air?   Now there was an indisputable executive recruiting triumph. I personally put that whole top executive team in place at Comanche Air when CA was losing 250 million dollars a month and, by God, they turned that company around in a year. True, they went out of the airline business. And, true, they paid off everyone including the shareholders five cents on the dollar when we took the company private. But when the dust cleared, Comanche Air emerged stronger than ever as Big Turtle Catering & Telecommunications, and the Big Turtle Board in gratitude made Cahoon and his guys probably the richest executive team in the country.

Big Turtle was a typical example of what G. B. Hume Associates could really do. Our unique combination of executive search know-how, insight into what makes a leader, and special psychological testing techniques almost always paid off. Our psychological testing alone was nearly infallible.   For instance, you ask a man whether he would prefer to dine with (a) Aristotle, (b) Fredrick the Great, (c) Donald Trump, or (d) Elvis Presley and that answer alone tells you about all you need to know. Or, at least, that was what our top shrink said and who would gainsay him? But I digress.

After I retired to our gated community in Sarasota, my life took on a fairly relaxed pattern. Each morning I would eat breakfast with Lillian on our patio overlooking the marina. Then I drove into town to buy the *New York Times* primarily for the bridge column and stopped by Morgan Stanley to check on my portfolio of tax free municipal junk bonds. Then I would drive back to the house for a rubber of bridge before lunch at the Carefree Club. After lunch, we played bridge until cocktails and dinner. After dinner, we always tried to squeeze in two or three rubbers before bedtime.

For the first year or so it was marvelous. Back inside my walled compound, I,

A King for America

as you would expect, did what I felt common sense dictated. I devoted myself to the perfection of my bridge game, a laudable and achievable objective.   Nothing tunes up your bridge game like playing eight or ten hours a day. I reveled in my increased prowess. But then, I must confess, I was beginning to become restive. Lillian is a large, commanding woman who would have done well running some dedicated enterprise such as a bomber command or naval strike force. Frankly no matter how much my game improved, her game was better, and once seated at a bridge table she can be extremely unforgiving. I found myself on more than one occasion looking across the table at her well-bred, horsey face and wondering if possibly I had retired too early.

In fact, it was at such a moment of reflection that our game was interrupted one early afternoon by a phone call from my former client, Cyrus Tower, the Philadelphia investment banker. It was, in truth, a terrible moment. Lillian had just made an opening demand bid of two spades; there was a pass to me; and I found that I had only three points in my hand. Nothing irritated Lillian more than for me to have garbage in my hand when she had a powerhouse. I felt deep distress.

"What do you say, partner," Lillian said interrupting my prolonged silence.

"I say…."   But, fortunately, I didn't have to say. A steward summoned me to the phone.

"Wulfie, this is Twitchie," Cyrus Tower said, using our old school names. "What the hell are you up to?"

"I'm trying to avoid answering Lily's demand bid," I said.

'No problem. I want you to come to Philadelphia immediately. We need you. The country needs you."

Spurred equally by patriotism and fear of responding to Lily, I did not hesitate. Two hours later I boarded Twitchie's private jet and was in Philadelphia by dinner time. We ate at Twitchie's town residence, an apartment overlooking Rittenhouse Square. On the walls of the long dining room hung Benjamin West portraits of Twitchie's most famous progenitor, Friendship Tower, and Friendship's sharp-faced wife, Merriment. Both had a look of obvious distaste. Possibly it was caused by the huge Jackson Pollock on the opposite wall.

There were only four of us for dinner. Twitchie, a tall thin man with kinky white hair and the weather-beaten face of a yachtsman, sat at the head of the table. As always, he radiated energy. He chain-smoked. He jammed his hands into the pockets of his Philadelphia Club blazer. He removed them. He laughed a lot. And he talked with the easy, self-assured tones of 300-year-old money.

Seated on Twitchie's right was a huge man with a soft, flabby well-used face and small hot brown eyes. I had never met him before, but, of course, I recognized him immediately. He was Lamar Wingate Tidibowl, then the Speaker of the United States

A King for America

House of Representatives. Win Tidibowl had been a congressman from Baton Rouge, Louisiana, for years and had become a major political force. He was among the handful of politicians most frequently mentioned as candidates for President.

Joe "Mr. Bob" Rantoon, the Speaker's chief of staff and ace political fixer, sat next to his boss and nursed a continually refreshed glass of Jack Daniels. He wore an unpressed white linen suit, looked as if he had been living in an old attic trunk, and spent most of his time in audit mode.

I sat on Twitchie's left and tried to make sense of what I was being told. Among the distractions were some excellent clear turtle soup and a marvelous Montrachet. For the record, the sole Albert also was superb, although I thought that the sauce was just a wee bit off the mark.

"Wulfie, you've gotta understand just how real fucked up this country is right now," Win Tidibowl said for the fourth time "I know you've been sitting down there in Florida on your 'ol ass in the sunshine not paying much attention, but we are in big trouble and Win Tidibowl is going to make you understand straight out why."

As was his wont, the Speaker in his colorful manner then described precisely the State of the Nation at that terrible time.   America's first Judeo-Irish president was serving the last dismal year of his first dismal term as President. He had been elected amid total political disarray by the Judeo-Irish Bloc on a one-issue platform: The granting of American Commonwealth status to a unified Ireland and Israel. He argued convincingly that the Irish were really one of the lost Tribes. Unfortunately, he failed to be equally convincing in summit negotiations between the Irish and Israeli leaders at what became the annual summit negotiating meetings at Camp David.

President Mandelbaum was equally inept in almost all other areas -- a pattern with which the American people had become comfortable in the first half of the 21st Century. When he entered office, U.S. foreign affairs, the military establishment, the economy, and the machinery of government were already in deplorable condition. In every case, sometimes only after enormous efforts, he had managed to make matters significantly worse.

As a personnel executive, I find it notable that Marvin's performance was no surprise to his wealthy family where he was affectionately known as Big Klutz. His older brother, Sean Irving Mandelbaum, had successfully withstood for 20 years all pressures to give Marvin a job, any job, in the family business, Plymouth Rock Fashions, a super conglomerate that owned retail chains, shopping malls, hotels and resorts all over the world. Election Day the entire family except for Marvin's wife, Tiffany, voted for his opponent. And, upon hearing that MOM as he wanted everyone to refer to him was elected, his grandmother and family matriarch, Mary O'Hara went directly to St. Patrick's Cathedral for a special two hour meeting with her personal confessor.

A King for America

"Understand where we are!" Win Tidibowl said again, rocking his large head back and forth. "The Bridge to the 22nd Century is there for all to see and, no surprise, all of those engineers who didn't have to learn how to add and all those other self-appointed political geniuses have made it a mite short. But no one really knows how bad things are, Wulfie. No matter how bad people think things are, I tell you they are worse."

Tidibowl thrust his face closer, forcing me to give up a few last bites of sole Albert. Tidibowl would not be denied the fullest attention.

"Our problem is we've let ourselves be softened up and Balkanized right into the crapper," Tidibowl said and pointed downward for emphasis. "In the old days in this country, all you had to do to get elected was worry about a few fat cats and the average American and a few special groups like the Irish and the Jews and maybe some blacks. Then we added the Hispanics and the Indians and the Asians and before you knew it in the name of diversity we had 55 hyphenated nationalities no one ever heard of who wanted their crazy languages taught in bilingual classes. And we had 40 religions who wanted their own national holidays and candle arrangements on the town mall. Then we had all these other groups: the tree huggers, the abortionists, the anti-abortionists, the friends of the sea turtles, the boys who liked boys,   the girls who liked girls, the real animal lovers. All of these groups multiplying like rabbits. And they all demand their "rights" and "fair shares" of a diminishing pie that our government bureaucracy has already eaten anyway. And our President can't even find the Men's Room on a clear day when he is not pumping for some cockamamie cause. Do I exaggerate, Mr. Bob?"

Mr. Bob smiled for the first time and rolled his eyes.

"But it's not really ol' Marvin's fault," Tidibowl continued. "Sure he's dumb. Shit, Marvin's about the dumbest white man I've ever met. But it's the system. Running countries calls for some privacy and free reign to twist some arms and make the best deals for all concerned.   You just can't do that anymore from the White House. Not even me, and I know how to coax the possums out of the woods better than most. But as my daddy used to say, there's no sense sending your best hog-caller when the pigs' ears are full of shit."

We contemplated this wisdom for a few moments in silence. Twitchie seemed to be waiting for me to ask a question, but I just continued to address myself to the remains of the wine.

"You know, I am sure, what will happen here in Philadelphia early next week?" Twitchie asked pointedly.

I shook my head and took another sip of the Montrachet.

"We have a Constitutional Convention. The first since 1797."

"Yes, yes," I said, now recalling. "The abortion issue. Isn't that the call of the convention?"

"That and green power and marrying your sister or your brother and universal food stamp debit cards and a lot of other kerfuffle," Win roared and threw up his hands. "But that's how we got the Convention called. Once called, I am happy to assure you, the original reason doesn't mean a pitcher of spit as my daddy used to say. Once called, the Convention can legally be open to any business brought before it. Thanks to Mr. Bob here, we have arranged to have the votes to make that happen."

"I gather that you have something in mind," I said, suddenly feeling the bridge player's growing excitement on sensing that his partner may after all have more than 15 points and a missing ace.

"Yes, sir," Win said. "Yes sir. At the right moment, I think we can make this Convention do something really important and just maybe save this country."

"May I ask what?"

"Absolutely. We're going to have a first class government that works for the first time in years. First we get rid of this crazy presidency and restore the monarchy. Then we get ourselves a Prime Minister who really runs the show like a statesman from the back room as smart prime ministers do. And we get ourselves up front a real classy fellow as King. Not like that last one we had, George III. He thought he was in charge. We want one who understands his main job is   to juice up   the crowds and appear on prime time on holidays. "

"May I presume that I am talking to our first Prime Minister?" I asked.

"Bet your ass."

"And who then would be King?"

"That's up to you. Twitchie says you're the best executive searcher in the business. Find a king for us. There have to be some good unemployed kings somewhere. But watch yourself. If this plan gets out, our enemies around the world who like this country flabby and compliant will try to stop us. Naturally we have taken the usual security measures."

I promptly cast myself into the tide of history.

LIVING HISTORY KING DISC-II

ROYAL AMERICAN HISTORICAL SOCIETY LIBRARY

As you might expect, my search for a king started in France.

The choice of starting point involved little genius on my part. After all, the country that purports to produce the finest wines, the finest chefs, the finest fashions, the finest memories of *la gloire,* the finest facades, that country certainly must produce the finest royal pretenders.

Besides, looking from an historical viewpoint at the options, France had to be among the more logical choices. The fact is that the great powers struggled with relative degrees of gross ineptitude for control of North America for three hundred years. I would say that in the Big Ineptitude Sweepstakes the British were probably the least inept of all. But the British would not do.   My client had already determined that a member of the British royal family would be most unacceptable in South Boston and the many other constituencies where "The Minstrel Boy" is still sung with fervor. Accordingly, I turned next to the French. Who would quarrel with their claim to being second least inept? Who, indeed?

I have always taken great pride in the boast that G.B. Hume Associates could hunt a head faster than any hunter in the business. Most executive search firms will spend endless amounts of time in preparation before even conducting interview Number One. They will study in great detail the organization into which the candidate is supposed to fit: Job responsibilities are analyzed; industry norms dissected; members of the executive team and their wives are quizzed by psychiatrists; the personal habits of the chief executive officer are explored; former employees are doggedly tracked to wherever they currently are located no matter how embarrassing. All of this data is then compounded into a big data working report that is often so frightening to everyone that it is impounded instantly.

There is no question that all of this activity is very worthwhile, particularly in justifying large fees and making everyone feel good about whomever is selected. On the other hand, we feel that we can justify equally large fees simply by promising not to bother everyone with all this rigmarole. Our approach is more pragmatic. I will tell you the secret. It consists primarily of asking our client one basic question: If you could fill your open position with anyone in the world, whom would you select? Then we get a bag of money and offer the job to that person. This approach may not always get you the best man, but it certainly saves a lot of time.

A King for America

Unfortunately, I found that our normal approach did not work as well when it came to locating likely kings. And there are good professional reasons. The talent pool in the king market has been dwindling for years. It's a perfect example of supply and demand. No one is out beating the bushes for a good king every day. As a result, there is very little interest among the young to go into the king business. Instead, as soon as they get out of college, they all want to take up being rock stars or mutual fund salesmen or investment bankers. Or, depending on their sexual propensities, opening an expensive restaurant full of exotic plants.

Moreover, I must confess I was not able to obtain very good direction from my client. When I asked Win Tidibowl the key question about which person in all the world he would like as king, he was certainly less than helpful. In fact, his response was rather crude. Apparently, you just don't meet too many kings around Baton Rouge, Louisiana.

"Wulfie, you just go out there and get us the best damn king you can find," Win told me. "This country deserves a first class king, you hear, not just one of those guys who sit around on their royal ass sucking up fancy drinks on some fat cat's yacht. I tell you, Wulfie, you got a challenge. Any real kings I've ever met I wouldn't hire to whistle up a taxi at a second-class hotel in Biloxi. But there must be one out there someplace who we wouldn't be ashamed to take around to introduce on Sunday afternoon after church."

With this kind of tight direction, I spent the next two days studying the *Almanach de Gotha*; made three lengthy overseas phone calls; and then booked myself on a 10 A.M. private jet to Paris. I checked into the Hotel Crillon in time to watch the opening of the Constitutional Convention on CNN. President Mandelbaum, appearing with the happy, bemused expression of the mentally challenged, was reading from his teleprompter:

"We are gathered here on the historic soil of Philadelphia, one of our great cities not yet in bankruptcy, to discuss amending our Constitution because of various issues that worry you. Now I strongly favor the inalienable right of every American to worry. On the other hand, some of us don't want to worry about anything. I favor that, too. But sad to say some of us worry about matters unnecessarily. There is a real problem I hope to correct."

I never learned what the President planned to do to end unnecessary worry because my secure smart phone rang. My long-time European operative, Marceline, called to confirm that I had arrived in Paris. By dinnertime, I was with her in the Crillon Grill sipping a moderately good Tattinger brut.

Marceline was a truly beautiful Frenchwoman in her early forties. She was the daughter of an industrialist from Lyon who had made millions of francs manufacturing a disgusting processed cheese called *Bon Bon Surprise*. She married and later divorced a certain Comte de Wagram who, although his title was barely Second Empire, had a rather cozy relationship with the *Tout Paris*. Subsequently, because the Comte had managed quite handily to spend most of her money, he disappeared and she opened a consulting firm for foreign businessmen interested in meeting important people in a reasonably social ambiance. The more social the ambiance, the higher her consulting fees. *Bien sur.*

Marceline and I must have made an unusual couple as we sat on a plush banquette in the Grill. Her costume, a silk pastiche of greens and reds with matching emeralds and rubies, exuded all the elegant simplicity that can only be achieved at the price of feeding a petit bourgeois family of four in Clermont-Ferrand for at least five years. As for myself, I noticed in an 18th Century mirror that I looked like an aging Bacchus packaged for shipment in wrinkled gabardine.

"Cher Wulfie," she said, "the candidate I have for you is *trés, trés extraordinaire.* He is simply superb. But, as you know, such a man is always one who doesn't need the job. And, after all, why should he take it?"

"The perks are very attractive," I suggested.

"Ah, but he would have to live in Washington, oui? Such a bore."

"He would not be there all the time. He would travel. And when he is there, he would live rather well. Better than most, I should say."

"Then, too, this large anonymous organization that he would have to head: Would there not be many problems?"

"Not at all. As I told you, his position would be purely ceremonial. That is why we don't really care if he has many brains. Although. I think, brains would be helpful, and for those I suppose we would pay extra. The key requirements are that he must have great style; he must have great bearing; there can be no scandal or, at least, nothing too unusual; and, above all, he must have a great aristocratic lineage tied in some way to North America."

"Then the man I have for you, I think, would be perfect. He is a direct descendent of Louis XV. His pedigree is superb. It looks like a history of Europe."

"That is a history that has not been all that great a success."

"But, you must admit it has had its moments."

"What is this man like?" I asked.

'*Charmant!* Attractive Mid-5O's. A full head of graying blonde hair. Good teeth. Rather fastidious. Bathes quite regularly for a Frenchman. Excellent physical shape. He used to play first class tennis but gave it up when it became popular, of course. Now he fences. He is also very successful in business in very much the American way. Is there a match?"

A King for America

"Perhaps. When do I see him?"

"Tomorrow, first thing. Ten o'clock."

I nodded approval and raised my glass.

"Tell me now, Wulfie, the name of this mysterious organization that our candidate would head in Washington," she said.

"Not at this time. My principals insist on secrecy. But believe me, it is very big. Think in terms of perhaps a country."

"Well, that certainly would be the size that would appeal to someone like..."

I held up a hand in warning and took another almond from the dish on the table in front of me. As I put the almond into my mouth, I carefully probed the dish with the forefinger of my left hand, winked at Marceline, and poured champagne into the dish. A spluttering sound and a distinct wisp of smoke came from the almonds.

"We must be careful," I said. "No names. As you can see, there was a microphone in one of the nuts."

The following morning I had a pleasant little breakfast in my room for seventy-five euros. As I had a second cup of coffee and a third croissant, I amused myself by looking out the window at the French trying to maim each other by driving at top speed through the Place de la Concorde. It was a beautiful summer day and traffic was heavy. Over toward the Pont de la Concorde a large black Citroen had mounted the trunk of a red Renault in what might prove to be one of the more interesting biological experiments of the decade. Only a hundred kilometers away a green Peugeot had collided with a Mercedes convertible apparently nearly decapitating its driver. The collision occurred at the foot of the Statue to Brest, almost the very spot where French enthusiasts had decapitated Louis XVI, an event that some in the executive search business might call the ultimate corporate out-placement.

Gazing at the historic site of Louis' final public appearance reminded me of my mission. I dressed and walked the few blocks to the Place Vendome where I took certain precautionary measures. The executive search business is always security conscious. On this assignment, particular concern was required. My destination, the Boutique Henri d'Artois, was directly across the square from the Hotel Ritz. First, I walked to the hotel, entered the lobby, and purchased a copy of the *Frankfurter Allgemeine Zeitung.* Then, while watching the front door, I inquired if Monsieur Pic were registered yet. Being assured that he was not and having assured myself that no one had followed me into the lobby, I departed and wandered casually three times around the square. Again, I felt certain no one had spotted me with the exception of the doorman.

"Pardon, Monsieur," he said on my third circumnavigation. "Are you lost?

A King for America

"Merci, Monsieur," I said adroitly in Berlitz French with a Swiss-German accent. "I am taking my morning walk while waiting for a friend."

"Bon chance, Monsieur," he said and bowed.

I felt that even if he were an agent that I obviously had him fooled and now even more casually I wandered back around the square. When I reached the boutique, I paused as if I were window shopping, acted as if I noticed something of interest, and strolled inside.

The front, room of the boutique was done entirely in two colors. The rugs, the drapes, the fittings, were in lime. The furnishings and walls were in orange. And everywhere were piled a cornucopia of lime and orange merchandise marked with the initials HA topped with a small crown. There were suitcases in 27 sizes, toiletry bottles and jars, four-foot scarves, two-foot long shoehorns, rug-size towels, African hunting hats, headbands, running shoes, picture frames, travel toilet tissue, bathroom scales, beach umbrellas, sauce and omelet pans, playing cards, picnic baskets, canvas chairs, and enormous stuffed bears wearing chic caps. A half-dozen attractive young women of various colors and all obviously suffering from serious dietary deficiency moved briskly among the mountains of things.

"I have an appointment with the Comte d'Artois," I told a tall black model who wandered by in a sheer lime dressing gown covered with orange HA's

"Henri is taking a shower," she said. "You may wait for him in his office."

I walked in the direction indicated and sat down in a small office totally dominated by crossed dueling sabers and epees on every wall. Ngo, a Vietnamese waiter wearing HA-initialed lime livery, carried in a silver cooler with a bottle of champagne and two glasses. Five minutes later a heavy-set man with damp graying hair emerged from a lime-tiled bathroom. He wore an orange silk dressing gown covered with lime HA's. On his feet, he wore gold-crested orange velvet pumps.

"Monsieur Hume," he said. "Let me present myself. I am, as you might suspect, Henri."

"And I assume Comte d'Artois as well?"

"Ah, yes, he shrugged. "And much more if you wish."

"I do, indeed. May I ask your full name?"

He sat down and poured champagne into our glasses.

"Is it important to this conversation?" he said, sounding bored.

"It is very important. In fact, that is an understatement."

A King for America

"Well, then, I am Henri Louis Phillipe d'Anjou et de Bourgogne, Duc de Bourbon, Comte de Charolais, Chevalier d'Antioch, Grande Seigneur de Martinique and d'Isles Ouest and so forth and so forth. But I prefer a simple Henri. After all, everyone knows who I am. But, if we are talking business, I do call myself the Comte d'Artois. It is quite legitimately one of my titles, of course, although dynastically it certainly is one of the tackier ones. After all, Artois is not Burgundy or Aquitaine, yes? Who would fight for it except the crazy Germans? However, my advertising agency, Le Syndicate d'Image Grand, tells me that Henri d'Artois has a certain ring to it. And, you know, being even a lousy count has some advantages in America and, of course, among the Japanese and the Arabs. Moreover, the HA monogram, especially with the little crown, is worth at least a 50 percent markup. Now, Monsieur Hume, do tell me what all this is about?"

"First, I must warn you that this is highly confidential and that there will be severe penalties for indiscretions.

"Such as?"

"There is a man known as Julius. He would undoubtedly arrange for you to have an unhappy accident if you were to engage in careless talk."

"Not really?"

"Oh, yes. He can be most persistent. On any given Tuesday you might receive a dozen frozen New York cut blow-up steaks. If you survive the devastation in your grill pit, Julius will introduce piranha fish into your Jacuzzi on Wednesday. Your copy of *Le Monde* will burst into flames on Thursday. A poisonous unguent will be rubbed on your opera glasses on Friday. In the end, you will gratefully eat a *soupcon* of deadly pâté merely for a little peace.

"All right, Monsieur," Henri said. "You have my word. I do not own a Jacuzzi, but I want to feel relaxed when I eat pâté. I will say nothing. Now, our mutual friend, Marceline, says that you have an opportunity for me of irresistible interest."

"Yes."

"Tell me about it."

"I represent a country that is looking for a very top executive.

"And what 'would his title be?"

"King."

"It must be a very small country. There is little demand for kings these days."

"On the contrary, it is a very big country. It is the United States."

"Monsieur, that is *formidable.* I think we should have another bottle of champagne."

Ngo returned immediately, almost falling through the door. It may have been only my natural suspicion of all Orientals who openly carry smart phones, but I felt certain that he must have been more than a waiter. However, I admit that the executive search business encourages a certain degree of paranoia.

"I must be impertinent," I told Henri as soon as Ngo departed and Henri refilled the glasses. "Just how good would you say are your titles?"

"Oh, the real stuff, Monsieur. The very best. I trace my line back to Philip the Good of Burgundy and his son, that con fini, Charles the Rash. You don't get to be a Chevalier d'Antioch, you know, sitting around in drafty castles. Someone had to get out there and chop up Saracens. There is hardly anything that has happened in this country for the last thousand years that at least one of my ancestors wasn't in there with the other royals swinging broadswords and raping peasant girls and all that neat stuff. If there were a restoration tomorrow, I can assure you I would have my very own set of keys to the Versailles washrooms."

"However," I said, "Marceline tells me that you are not active in royalist circles. May I inquire why?"

Henri threw his arms in the air and rolled his eyes. As he continued to talk, he casually removed an epee from a nearby wall and flicked its thin blade idly at various objects about him.

"My relatives do not like me," he said. "They do not approve of my business activities. You may ask why? I will tell you a secret. The smart money is not betting on a restoration this month in this country. Therefore, I leave the royalty business to my relatives and continue to make good friends with the Banque de Paris. For example, take my designer business. It is superb. We sell perfectly terrible but fashionably overpriced clothes in boutiques on three continents. Lime and orange, Monsieur, is recognized throughout the world as my trademark even without the HA's. And Henri Enterprises also has greatly diversified. We franchise throughout France 650 L'Escargot Quik restaurants. Today there is not a major town in France where you cannot stop at a lime and orange L'Escargot Quik for a less than memorable meal. And my latest venture is La Vacance Sexy -- packaged trips to once great if now somewhat sleazy vacation spots around the world. We are positively benefactors. For as little as 1000 francs a salesgirl at the Bon Marche department store in Paris can be laid on a fun weekend in the Auvergne by an over-tipped bellboy from the Hotel George V. My relatives, I fear, do not identify with these worthwhile social endeavors."

Henri laughed and made a vicious thrust with his epee and pierced a lampshade. A number of holes in the lampshade indicated that it was a favorite target.

"How do you think that they would feel about your becoming a king?"

A King for America

"Far better than I," he said. "Once they got over their shock and blind envy, I am certain they would be ecstatic. They would descend on Washington en masse. After all, what else do these poor people have to do these days? The royalty business consists primarily of attending the baptisms, weddings and funerals of their relatives. And, of course, there are a lot of these events because over the years everyone has married his cousin or worse. But, you know, after a while certain tedium sets in. It is not the same as running governments no matter how badly. So there would be great joy, I am sure. My wife, the Princess Victoria Sophie, would be happiest of all. She is a terribly suspicious woman. She thinks I spend too much time working late with my models. Unfortunately, she has no appreciation of the pressures of this business, But…"

He stopped momentarily, and this time the epee swung around and touched my Chest.

"But," he repeated, "the true question, my friend, is why on earth you would seek a Frenchman for this job. After all, we have really done so poorly at these things. All that rubbish about gloire on which that con superior, DeGaulle, used to get himself tipsy: The man just never knew the truth. But, after all, why would he? At best, his ancestors spent their lives poaching game or worse. My family really knew. They should have. As I told you, they were always there. They were among the people who, as the saying goes, invariably screwed things up."

"You exaggerate," I demurred, "Surely, you exaggerate."

"Not at all. Go back to the 13th Century. Start at Crecy. That was as good a total disaster as any. What did the King of France and all his royal cousins including my relatives do? They charged the English bowmen. It was a beautiful thing to see, of course. Unfortunately, it was also fatal. Sixty years later, we did it again at Agincourt. Only, since it didn't work on horseback at Crecy, we tried it on foot. The debacle came quickly. France went down for a century."

The Comte shook his head sadly and continued his monologue.

"As for our royal rights in America, it is sufficient to say that four hundred years later French gloire was still up to its usual performance. We owned Canada. But on the Plains of Abraham at Quebec, simply put, the army of Louis XV marched into the British guns of that German carpetbagger, George II. When the smoke cleared, not only Quebec but all French Canada was down the tube. We still owned Louisiana: a third of the continent. But Napoleon, our greatest general, was no better in the end.   Although he certainly provided us with a fun decade, he was a truly world class loser and. he sold Louisiana to you Americans for carfare. Since then it's been all downhill. Consider that in the last hundred years we have fought three wars with Germany and they have proven without doubt only that the Germans know how to get to Paris."

"I insist again that you do yourself a disservice," I said "Look how much worse others have done."

A King for America

"That is true. Look at the Russians and the Italians and the Spanish."

"Precisely. If not a Frenchman, then whom?"

"A good question, but at any rate, now that I think about it, not me. After all I already have plenty of gloire as it is. Have you seen the latest edition of L'OK?'

I shook my head and he speared with his epee a glossy magazine from a pile of papers on a nearby table. The cover depicted two fun-loving young women painting cartoons on their stomachs with magic markers.

"Here it is," he said happily, opening the magazine to a full-page picture of himself surrounded by models in lime and orange string bikinis. The article was called:

THE COMTE BUILDS AN EMPIRE

"Why would I give up an empire?" he said, laughing, and playfully flicked a button from my jacket.

"Possibly for an American crown" I suggested, picking up my button.

I was not at all put out. As we all know in the head hunting biz, the good candidates always play hard to get.

LIVING HISTORY KING DISC-III

ROYAL AMERICAN HISTORICAL SOCIETY LIBRARY

But I could not pin all my hopes on the possibility that the Comte would change his mind. I needed more candidates and moved on to that traditional royal playground on the French Riviera in search of leads. As always when in this part of the world, I checked into to one of the better suites at the Negresco where I waited for several days to be granted a meeting with the aging Grand Duke Alexei Nikolaevich.

Meantime, back in Philadelphia, the Constitutional Convention appeared to be moving as planned by the Speaker. As I sat in my suite looking out over the Mediterranean, I read in the *International Herald Tribune:*

> PHILADELPHIA – Deadlocked delegates at the Second Constitutional Convention today dropped all original calls for amendments and embraced a new plan to restructure the federal government.
>
> A Committee of the Whole chaired by House Speaker Lamar W. Tidibowl approved an amendment that would vest total executive authority in a Prime Minister and promote the Office of President to constitutional King.
>
> If approved by the full convention, the amendment must be confirmed by three quarters of the states to become law.
>
> President Marvin Mandelbaum, who opposed the amendment, predicted it would not survive.

Other major stories on the front page were what one had come to expect. One headline said:

NORTH KOREA MISSILES IN ECUADOR;

US SENDS PYONGYANG TESTY NOTE

Another said:

ISLAMIST MILITIA TRADE

KIDNAPPED SAUDI SHEIK

FOR SIX F-18s AND PARTS

A King for America

The Grand Duke Alexei Nikolaevich lived on Cap Ferrat in a small elegant villa surrounded by a park. The park sat on a small promontory jutting languidly into the Mediterranean. Most days one could sit there on a bench (the park was open to the public for an hour Monday through Friday afternoons for tax purposes) and watch pleasure craft laden with cocaine and other leisure products arrive from Turkey and North Africa. The park, itself, was filled with exotic flowers and the Grand Duke's famous collection of talking birds. The birds sat in trees to which they were attached by long golden chains. The air was perfumed by flowering shrubs and by a small man who walked through the park twice daily with a spray gun filled with *L'Heure Bleu*, reputed to have been a favorite of the late Dowager Empress.

The Grand Duke Alexei and I sat in a gazebo overcrowded with ferns and gardenias growing in K'ang Hsi urns. At the time of our meeting he could have been no less than 86. His tall and very thin body seemed to be hiding in a dark blue suit of a vaguely Edwardian cut. His fine elongated face appeared to have been drying in a closet for a long time. It bore the distinctive marks of much history gone awry. His large eyes were warm with sorrows forgotten and the promise of his daily bouquet of small exquisite treats and household pleasures. Nothing surprised or excited him; perhaps nothing ever had. We sipped tea poured from a heavy baroque silver samovar and talked about his collection of Faberge jeweled eggs. A plate of small rich cakes each frosted with a crown sat on the table in front of us.

"The eggs have been a great source of amusement and support in my old age," he said. "My Faberge egg factory just over the border in Italy has been far more successful than I could have hoped. Every year we find at least one new royal egg and issue a limited edition of 20,000. I personally sign the authenticating certificates with my seal."

"A most generous touch, Highness," I said. "You obviously bring much pleasure to many."

He bowed his distinguished white head and dismissed the subject with his right hand on which he wore a large gold and onyx ring engraved with the double imperial eagle.

"You know, Mr. Hume, since my fourth heart attack I no longer go out in society," he said. "I hear so little firsthand. You say America now has great problems?"

"None, Highness, that cannot be cured with strong leadership," I essayed carefully and offered the warm confiding smile of the head hunter.

"Well, that certainly would exclude the Romanovs," he said. "They have led nothing successfully for 200 years."

"You are modest, Highness. I look upon your family as a sleeping tulip bulb waiting only the right opportunity."

A King for America

The Grand Duke nodded appreciatively and poured more tea.

"Rule Britannia!" shouted a large blue bird that occupied one of the flowering trees just outside the gazebo.

"Well, of course," the Grand Duke said, ignoring the bird, "when you put it like that I suppose we might have someone around who might give it a try. Not my nephew, Sergei. He's much too drunk most of the time. And I shouldn't think you would want the Grand Duke Dimitri. He sells Fiats in Nice and, because he is much too stupid to lie about them, he naturally is starving. Anyway he is much too close to the Heir and always expects to move back to Tsarkoye Selo at any moment. But Prince Alexander might do. He is truly quite clever. He has made a lot of money in Monte Carlo selling condominiums and mutual hedge funds of questionable value."

"Vive la France:" shouted another nearby bird with an orange bill shaped like a shovel.

"Do you think Prince Alexander would listen to a proposition?" I asked.

"Oh, indeed. He will always do that. Just bring a lot of money. He has very expensive tastes. In truth, I understand that some of them are also rather bizarre. That, I suppose, could cause you a problem in Washington."

"Oh, I doubt that. At least, not in Washington."

"Well, then, talk to the Prince by all means. It's really an exciting idea. The Russians won't like it much, I'm sure. They've never been fond of us even after all these years since the Revolution. Let bygones be bygones, I say. But no, they keep worrying, worrying, worrying about people like me running back to Russia to occupy old palaces."

The Grand Duke laughed and ate a little cake with enormous relish.

"Good God," he exclaimed and crossed himself backwards, "who would want to live there under those pseudo czars even with all the Soviet Communist monsters dead or senile? Still no decent bathrooms, no proper servants, and all that perfectly terrible cooking and bad vodka. An hour at Cap Ferrat for a cycle in St. Petersburg or whatever they call it these days, I say. You know I hear that all the really good caviar is exported and the last decent bottles of champagne were drunk by the German General Staff on the retreat from Moscow in '43. Tell me, dear Mr. Hume, who but a madman would go back?"

"Deutschland über alles:" called a black and red bird from a medium sized ginkgo.

"Just how close is Prince Alexander to the Throne?" I asked.

A King for America

"Sixth or seventh, I should say, depending on whether you count Old Style or New Style. A very good claim really if this were 1905 when blowing up Romanovs was such popular sport. But today he really has no chance of inheriting unless everyone died at once of what I presume would be diagnosed as total boredom. Not, of course, that any of the others have any chance of inheriting either. But they keep busy."

"Doing what?"

"Oh, a thousand things: granting new titles, awarding new medals, writing unwanted letters of advice to their few remaining crowned cousins. There is no end to it. It keeps a man off the streets. You would be surprised how many people want a title or a medal even when it has a promissory note attached. Honestly now, do you really think that your countrymen would like a king who did these things?"

"Why not"

"So complicated, you know. So undemocratic, too, come to think of it. All that court etiquette. I can remember when I was a boy hearing the complaints of my grandfather, the Grand Duke Vladimir. How it bored him getting the Czar up in the morning; standing around watching him eat eight course meals; tucking him in at night. Things were less formal under Uncle Nicky, of course, but that was probably the problem. Poor silly Nicky. Once you start letting down the barriers there's no stopping. Queen Victoria knew that. I'm convinced that the only thing that kept her alive so long was the thought of Bertie sitting around with his hunting boots off and his trousers unbuttoned, so to speak."

"I think that Americans do secretly love a lord," I said.

"Really? Maybe on parade. But in the White House flogging servants for forgetting to bow three times while backing out of the East Room may be a bit much."

"Do your servants do that?"

"Naturally. But they still have native cunning. They know what's best for them. Most Americans don't know that anymore, do they?"

"I think Americans are more ready for royalty than you may think. They've been trained for it by our great corporations."

"The consumers, you mean?"

"No, no. The top executives. They have been working on backing out of rooms with great style for years."

"Then truly you should talk to Prince Alexander. You can find him any day at lunch at the Hotel de Paris in Monte Carlo. Get there before the check and he will welcome you."

""So, you do think he will be interested?"

"Well, if nothing else, he most certainly will be interested to know the basis on which he might make a legitimate claim."

"Oh, that's easy. Russia owned Alaska and the Alaskans are always complaining that they are left out of everything. Nothing is so important in America as satisfying a minority complaint."

"Is it true that Alaska also has much oil?"

"Absolutely."

"Then Prince Alexander will indeed be interested."

"God bless America," shouted a red and blue parrot that had flapped to the roof of the gazebo.

"Life to the Czar, "said the Grand Duke to no one in particular.

A King for America

ROYAL AMERICAN HISTORICAL SOCIETY LIBRARY

My assiduous but genteelly relaxed executive search regrettably underwent rapid acceleration following my most pleasant meeting with the Grand Duke. I have never liked to bustle through life. There are too many of the little pleasures that one will surely miss. Here a superb deuce de sole homardine; there a great Margaux; here an undiscovered El Greco; there an exquisite private garden; here a supreme de volaille Gabriel; there a caneton Tour d'Argent.

Well, you understand, of course. Bustle and sense of urgency mess life up every time. Look at what it did to England in World War II.

However, on occasion the pressures of the world do relentlessly intrude. And, as in this case, when they intrude rudely and insistently, one must pay heed.

I returned from Cap Ferrat to the Negresco where I planned to review my strategy and notes and enjoy the weather for a few more days before pressing forward. You can understand, therefore, why I was considerably put out to be intruded upon by a phone call from Mr. Bob. I was just beginning a quite adequate breakfast of fresh blood oranges, oeufs brouilles Princess Marie and the four or five small crusty croissants on which I always insist. My table had been laid most beautifully in the sunshine by a window overlooking a Ming blue sea.

"Good God,' I told him, 'it must be the middle of the night in Washington. Here it's barely dawn. Can't a man eat a roll in peace before going to his daily labor?"

"My watch says 6 A.M. I do apologize," Mr. Bob said. "Apparently the sun comes up damn late in Nice. I know how busy you must be, but the Speaker and I have a little problem. Developments here are moving fast. The states are all falling in line. Legislatures in the final six will confirm the amendment this week. That means a Congressional Search Committee will be set up in no time. We need our candidate ready to put on a crown."

"I don't understand. How do you know they'll all confirm the amendment?"

"Because we paid in cash. And out man Julius took care of any dissenters. Now do you understand?"

"Yes, yes,' I said, trying to get a mouthful of my eggs before they chilled. "But even so these things can't be hurried much. There are many, many complications."

'We're all going to have many, many complications if we don't have our king standing in the royal wings. We don't want a lot of right-thinking, amateur help here in making the selection. And, we have some reason to believe that some of the nastier elements of the foreign competition may be getting on to this, too."

"Impossible,' I said, carefully buttering a croissant. "I have been most discreet."

"I'm sure,' Mr. Bob said. "Probably the spooks got it all wrong as usual. Anyhow, Wulfie, step on the gas, you hear now. Your country's counting on you."

Before I could swallow my morsel of croissant and say more, he rang off. There was nothing else to do but plunge ahead. I would have to cancel my plans for spending the day in the Cote d'Azure galleries and possibly a pleasant drive into the hills to St. Paul de Vence for lunch. Such are the penalties of my trade.

I finished breakfast in gloom, dressed, and put in a call to the Hotel de Paris in Monte Carlo to make a luncheon reservation there. I would have to meet with Prince Alexander immediately; then decide on my next move. The maitre d'hotel graciously took my reservation; then the pressures of the world made a new intrusion.

"Perhaps you know what time the Prince Alexander will be having lunch today?" I asked as casually as possible.

'Unfortunately, he will not be with us today, Monsieur," the maitre d'hotel said.

'I thought he had lunch with you every day.'

"Yes, but unfortunately that is finished. We are very sorry. It is because of the accident.'

"What accident? Something in the kitchen?'

"No, no, certainly not. It is because of the accident on the Grande Corniche. The Prince's Lotus apparently had a technical difficulty on one of the sharper curves. What can I say?"

"When did this happen?" I asked with considerable trepidation.

'Yesterday afternoon, Monsieur. Shortly after lunch. I saw him leave myself in the best of spirits. I remember so well because his car was brought around from the garage by an attendant whom I had not seen previously. A short wiry foreigner with an eyepatch. He said his name was Dimitri. I assumed he worked for the Prince.'

I cancelled my reservation, of course. Very regrettable. I had been looking forward to the Paris' poulet grille sauce diable, but obviously it would be best to get away from the area at least for the present.

I had written the week before through contacts in the Bundesbank to Otto, Margrave of Upper Oldenburg-Schleswig-Gotha. I had planned to visit the Margrave the following week in Munich. I now hastily arranged an afternoon flight and sought by phone to meet with him as early as possible. I was in luck. The Margrave invited me to lunch with him the following day. Nothing pleases me more than when I can combine my passion for both the table and the hunt.

The Margrave, through his family papers and connections along with a lifetime of study, was unquestionably one of the leading royal genealogists of Europe. It is true that Otto, who was known in the popular German press as the Merry Margrave of Munich, had certain eccentricities. These included sudden fits of Bavarian melancholia and a great fondness for jockeys. But these in no way interfered with his devotion to aristocratic history and to following the activities of hundreds of extant royals. His files had become massive and currently were maintained in the small ballroom of the Residenz, a massive pile of a palace that King Ludwig I of Bavaria had rebuilt in the center of Munich during the last century. Otto also lived in the palace in a grace and favor apartment and when not working on his research was known to indulge his interest in the racetrack there. According to my Paris agent, Marceline, Otto would spend much time in the glass enclosed winter Garden on the roof of the Residenz where he would wander hand in hand with one or two of his jockey friends, inspecting the exotic flowers that bloomed under a vast glass covering that was shaped liked a Greek cross, or sometimes they would float idly in a gondola on the small lake and discuss betting odds.

As you would expect after the unpleasantness on the Grande Corniche, I approached the Residenz with great circumspection. I checked into the Hotel Vier Jahreszeiten under the name Millard Fillmore and loudly asked if I had received any calls from Herr Schmitt of the Society for Prevention of Cruelty to Animals. I also asked the concierge to mail a postcard to my niece, Millicent, in Erie, Pennsylvania, promising to buy her more German march records. Then I ate a quiet dinner in my room.

The following morning I remained at the hotel until 10:30. Before leaving, I again casually inquired about a call from Mr. Schmitt; acted annoyed that I had not heard from him; and walked a few blocks to Cook's. There I boarded a Fuji Fun Vacations tour bus for the Alte Pinakothek and the Residenz Museum. A large group of sincere Japanese tourists and I looked at paintings in the Pinakothek for more than an hour and I bought a postcard of Tintoretto's "Vulcan Surprising Mars and Venus." Finally, we reboarded our bus and arrived at the Residenz Museum a few minutes before noon. The guide led us directly to the former Throne Room where he delighted the group by agreeing to the taking of pictures. During the ensuing explosions of light I ducked behind a large Chinese vase, moved quietly down a hall, and told a guard dressed like a 19th Century Imperial Cavalry officer that I had lost my way.

"Show me immediately to the apartment of the Margrave of Upper Oldenburg," I ordered sharply. "The Margrave is expecting me.'

"Ja wohl, mein Herr,' the guard shouted, clicked his heels, and led me through a door hidden behind a 15th Century tapestry depicting the pillaging of Salzburg. The guard led me up a private stairway, down a corridor lined with armor, across an interior courtyard used to store broken statuary, and into an elevator cage barely big enough for me.

'Drei," the guard said, clicked his heels, and shut the elevator door.

"Danke,' I said, curtly nodded, and pushed the elevator button. The elevator made a sick whirring noise, jerked upward into darkness, shuddered, and stopped. I opened the gate and stood before an ornate stained glass door emblazoned with the arms of Upper Oldenburg: Thirty-two quarterings on a field of orange topped with a bored-looking lion and two equally bored Rhine maidens. Beneath the arms was the motto LORBE POR TEMPUM. I believe it comes from a memo that Cicero sent to Mark Antony in Egypt. Liberally translated, of course, it means 'stall for time.'

I pulled the bell and a heavily bearded butler wearing medals on his dress coat opened the door. A moment later I was ushered into the presence of the 21st Margrave of Upper Oldenburg-Schleswig-Gotha.

Otto was standing in the middle of his heavily over-furnished drawing-room. He was of medium height and of indeterminate middle age. His dark hair was full and cut stylishly in layers. His face was young looking and quite pink behind a silver pair of pince nez attached to a black silk ribbon. He was dressed for the country. He wore a smartly cut hacking jacket and green whipcord trousers. He spoke English with an accent that could have been acquired only from a tutor or a British public school. He also had a slight stutter.

"Ah, H-Hume," the Margrave said. "Good of you to join me for lunch."

"Good of you to have me," I said. "Very short notice.'

The Margrave simultaneously acknowledged the truth of my comment and brushed it aside with a gesture.

"Just as long as you have taken proper precautions,' he said. 'It w-was awfully naughty what h-happened to poor Alexander.'

"You have heard the unfortunate news," I said with a lowered tone that I hoped was sufficiently funereal.

"It was certainly un-fff-fortunate for Alex. Such an attractive chap. B-But how would you appreciate the delicate sensitivities of the Russians in these matters? So jumpy about Romanovs. It is just as well that you have come to me as soon as possible. Herr Kron from the Bundesbank has explained all t-t-to me."

"Herr Kron, I assume, has then certainly discussed with you our readiness to extend a generous financial consideration to you or an appropriate charity in return for your assistance in this matter."

"Oh, yes, y-y-yes,' the Margrave said, nodding and half whinnying. "Normally, of course, there would be no question of a charity. The m-m-money would come to me. But, in this case, dear H-Hume, it is not expected. I do so want to help. I should certainly be related to almost anyone you chose unless he's a Turk and I can't wait to visit W-W-Washington as a member of the royal family. Come, let us talk about it at lunch.'

Otto took me by the arm and guided me through one of the room's great rococo doors into a small dining room. Windows on one wall looked out over a formal garden that needed clipping. The other wall was dominated by a full length portrait of Lola Montez, the famous 19th Century Spanish dancer and favorite of King Ludwig I.

"Charming," the Margrave said, nodding toward the portrait. 'But I w-would never have given up the throne for her the way Ludwig did. Then, of course, I have broader tastes. However, it does make a point. You do not want a Wittelsbach like Ludwig for America. T-T-Too eccentric. I am sure you agree that your candidate must not be t-t-too eccentric?"

Otto did not wait for a response but rang a small golden bell for the bearded servant to serve lunch and talked on.

"And you c-c-certainly don't want a Hohenzollern. Although you know, there is a precedent. You Americans once wrote to Prince Henry of Prussia, he was the brother of Frederick the Great of all people, and asked Henry if he would consider being king. The letter was written in 1786. The terrible Hessians had barely gone home. Henry apparently preferred the joys of Prussia whatever those may be and turned down the offer. Good thing, too. You wouldn't want the Hohenzollerns running around Washington insisting that everyone change uniforms 16 times a day."

He paused to sip some wine. It was an excellent Mosel. Certainly a Bernkasteler-Doktor.

'I h-hope you like it,' he said, making it clear that whether I liked it or not was a matter of complete indifference to him. 'It's just something local."

"The Wittelsbach and Hohenzollern claims to an American throne also are both rather thin anyway, are they not?" I ventured.

"P-P-Precisely. Of course, we can always prove anything through collateral bloodlines, b-but you need something stronger. That's why, d-dear chap, most of the German minor states are not for you. Schwarzburg-Rudolstadt, Mecklenburg-Schwerin, Lippe: all so helpful when one is looking for really good blood and no political problems. After all, who cares about Schwarzburg-Rudolstadt. B-But also who would really buy the proposition that the American monarchy should be r-r-restored by someone from the House of Schleswig-Holstein-Sonderburg-Gluckersburg just because he is a seventh cousin twice removed of George of Hanover and England? No, my dear friend, we must d-do something a little less obscure."

I chewed slowly a fine piece of veal, drank some more wine, and waited to see where we were going.

'The French, of course, h-have a strong claim,' he continued. " Frankly, I find them and the whole idea of one of them on an American throne quite detestable, but I cannot deny it. If it had not been for their own morbid interest in blowing up Italians and Belgians, America would have been mostly French as we all know. But what can you expect of a country that invented the bourdalue? Think of the glory of it: a triumph in Sévres porcelain dedicated to the needs of weak female kidneys. I understand that you have been talking to the Comte D'Artois. Well, there you are. His claim to the throne would be rather first rate, of course. He can trot out all those early Dukes of Burgundy and other historic miscreants and make an excellent story of it. B-But, you know, in the end do you r-r-really want a designer of overpriced women's clothes for a king? I say, my dear Hume, that would be a bit thick."

"Where then does that leave us?" I asked, nodding to the servant when he offered to fill my glass. "No French, no English, no Russians, no Germans

"N-Not far from a s-s-solution. Your idea to look at a Burgundian was not far off the mark, but you did not look in the right place. You should have gone to their relations in Vienna instead of P-Paris.'

"A Habsburg!" I said, not so much in astonishment but as a means of showing I was not totally ignorant of imperial nesting grounds.

'Exactly, my dear Hume. A H-Habsburg would have it all, you see. The very best blood, oh the very, very best. And the very best claim, too. Along with all their other possessions, the Habsburgs owned Spain. And the Spanish were there in America first of all. No one wants to remember that, I know. But even after the first American monarchy was dispatched at Yorktown, the Spanish still owned most of the continent including the Sunbelt. I tell you a H-H-Habsburg would be superb."

'Do you really think so? I must confess it gives me a problem. They really haven't much of a reputation for brains or even common sense -- at least not for the last three or four centuries. All those auto-da-fe's and bullfights, all those bad military decisions and wetbacks: not a very good press."

'Good G-G-G-God, Hume," the Margrave shouted. "Brains? Common sense? Who is talking about that? We are talking about b-b-b-blood. We are talking about pure l-l-legitimacy. There we have the best. You don't want brains in a king. That's not the j-j-job. It hasn't been for a long time."

"I take it that you have someone in mind,' I essayed and silently toasted him and Lola Montez.

"I do, indeed,' Otto said, straightening his back proudly. "And you will be surprised. He is closer to home than you th-th-th-think."

LIVING HISTORY KING DISC-V

ROYAL AMERICAN HISTORICAL SOCIETY LIBRARY

The prime candidate that the Margrave had in mind was the Archduke Philip Maximilian Leopold Francis von Habsburg. And, I must say, his biography was impressive. Sipping an after-lunch glass of champagne, the Margrave with considerable pomp in his voice read to me from the *Almanach de Gotha* and *Who's Who* while interjecting personal asides.

"Direct descendant of Charles V (1500-58), Holy Roman Emperor, King of Spain, King of Germany, lord of all Spanish possessions in the New World, down through Archduke Maximilian (18xx-18xx), younger brother of Emperor Francis of Austria-Hungary. Maximilian, Emperor of Mexico, formerly New Spain, assassinated. His Empress Carlotta, mentally unbalanced to say the least, escaped to her father, King of Belgium. Maximilian' s son, Leopold, the Archduke Philip's great grandfather, escaped to the former Spanish colonial capital, Santa Fe, where he settled with the help of Spanish aristocratic landowners. Leopold became a millionaire copper baron. His son, Ferdinand, spent most of the money after moving to New York. Ferdinand's son, Francis, went to West Point and rose to colonel, retired to Switzerland where he died in his 90's in a mysterious hotel fire. Which brings us to his son, our candidate, the Archduke Philip."

"And where and what is he?" I asked.

"The Archduke has always been a man of modest means and aristocratic pretensions. He taught ancient history for many years at several fashionable boys' schools before retiring to a small town in the Upstate New York. I have never had the pleasure of meeting him, but, according to my American contacts, he is a tall, elegant looking man in his 60's. Never married. Absolutely no scandal."

"Wouldn't a king without an heir be a problem?"

"Not in this case. There are always plenty of unemployed royals with connected bloodlines to choose from once you have someone firmly on a throne. And who knows what a vigorous king might produce?"

"Tell me again why you think this candidate is so exceptional."

"The b-b-bloodlines are excellent. You really can't do much better than being descended from Holy Roman Emperor Charles V. He ran Europe, you know, and he owned at one time or another m-m-most of what is now the United States. He and his descendants are related to every royal family of importance. And we have the tie to the unfortunate Emperor of Mexico. For Philip, becoming King of America with its huge

Hispanic population, would, I should think, m-m-make his arrival something of a homecoming."

"I thought the Mexicans shot his great great grandfather because they didn't want him around."

"Water under the d-dam. And, I am sure you would agree, Maximilian really did not play his cards well. He listened too much to Carlotta and that buffoon, Napoleon III, and you know what happened to him."

"If we decide to go ahead, how do you think Philip will take this opportunity?"

The Margrave laughed. "My good man, d-don't be naive. Very seldom have I seen or heard of a royal who when offered a throne did not begin to salivate. Some, of course, do go to work either out of necessity or to keep their sanity while pretending to put thrones in the past. However, I assure you that no matter how much boredom Philip exhibits about matters royal he will be very interested in what you have to say."

"Well, the position does include reasonably decent compensation and some very good benefits."

"And I gather the workload is not too difficult."

"No. According to the job description, all the heavy lifting will be performed by the new Prime Minister."

"Ah," the Margrave said knowingly and refilled our glasses. "Under those circumstances Philip would be perfect. So different from his father, the colonel. He always wanted to be doing something. I knew him very well. We worked together on some matters during the Cold War."

"I see. Is that how he ended up roasted in that hotel fire?"

"Possibly. The old KGB could be so unpleasant."

I nodded understandingly, sipped my champagne and made my decision.

"What is the next step in proceeding with the Archduke?"

"I will contact him for you, inform him that you would like to call on him to discuss a very important family matter, recommend that he see you. I can do all this on one of my secure phones. Be assured no one will know."

"And if he agrees to a meeting where will that be?"

"I recommend that you call on him as a friend at his home. I understand he lives in a charming gatehouse on one of the old river estates near a little town named Rhinebeck on the Hudson River, only a couple of hours drive north from New York."

A King for America

"I think I've driven through it," I said. "It's not far from Franklin Roosevelt's mansion at Hyde Park."

"Too bad he's no longer alive," the Margrave said. "I think he would have loved this job we're talking about. Without the Prime Minister, of course."

The Margrave made his promised phone call on a secure line that evening and reported that Philip was appropriately disbelieving but interested. I flew the next day to New York where I had a Mercedes M-Class SUV and a driver waiting for me to take me to Rhinebeck for my scheduled meeting the following morning. That gave me some time to poke around the locals for any intelligence about the Archduke.

Sitting in the rear of the Mercedes under a robe, I fell asleep. But somewhere north of Poughkeepsie as we drove through Hyde Park, the driver, a young fellow decorated with 5 PM shadow in the current fashion, said: "May I ask you a question?"

"Sure," I said, warily.

"I'm a graduate of Yale with top marks. Why the hell am I driving a cab?"

"I assume because you haven't found a better job. What is your field?"

"I took a lot of crapo studies courses but I have a graduate degree in archeology."

"Well, as a specialist in executive placement, I certainly understand your problem. There simply isn't a big demand for archeologists. Maybe you should consider finding a more marketable specialty."

"Liike driving a cab?"

"Don't jest. Did you know that Commodore Vanderbilt started out running a boat between Staten Island and Manhattan? We just passed one of his family's smaller mansions. A bright fellow such as you could start out driving a cab and end as taxi czar of New York."

"Not with that joker Mandelbaum in the White House. Is this one lousy world or what?"

"Don't despair. I think better times are coming."

Ten minutes later we arrived in Rhinebeck and pulled up in front of the Beekman Arms, an old colonial tavern. I dispatched my wannabe archeologist for the night, checked in, showered; changed for dinner, and wandered into the inn's tap room. It was empty except for two local regulars watching an unusually dopey-looking blonde news anchor named Mitzie on the bar TV.

"First trlp to Rhinebeck?" the bartender asked as he poured a sparse Scotch.

"Just passing through," I said. "Stopping long enough to visit a friend. Philip Habsburg. Maybe you know him?"

"Sure. Comes in here with his big dogs. Very polite gentleman. Very active with the preservationist crowd."

"I can do a without his goddam dogs," Regular One said. "They smell."

"Of course, they smell," Regular Two said. "They're otter hounds."

"But I don't have to smell them."

"Pentagon sources downplayed the size of the nuclear warheads sold to the Nigerians," Mitzie was saying with a non-sequiter smile. "The State Department called on the U.N. to investigate."

"I've never been to Philip's house. Is it far from here?" I asked.

"Ten minutes," the bartender said. "Over on the River Road. He lives in the gatehouse at the Randolph place."

"He got his friends the Colonial Preservation Society to fix up that gatehouse as a town project but the manor house is a wreck," Regular One said. "No one has lived there since old Randolph fell down the stairs and broke his neck."

"Your friend' Phil, rents the gatehouse from old Randolph's nutty cousin," Regular Two said.

"She's not so nutty" the bartender said. "She lives in one of the Livingston mansions up on the river and she got the state to pay for restoring it as a national treasure."

"Didi, his long-time companion, told Chicago police she found Gunga Z, the drug boss, with a knife in his chest in the shower," Mitzie was saying, still smiling. "There was no blood because the shower was on."

"Typical la-de-da preservationist scam," Regular One said. "You got the right ancestors, you get the money."

"Well, Phil there must have a room full of them," Regular Two said. "You know, they call him 'Duke.' But what's he Duke of I always ask."

"Congressman Gilbert Tokay denies using two million dollars in campaign funds to buy a summer home in the Cayman Islands," Mitzie was saying, dropping the smile for accusatory pursed lips.

A King for America

"You having dinner here in the bar?" the bartender asked me.

"No, I think I'll eat in the diningroom." I said.

I checked out of the Beekman Arms shortly before 10 o'clock. My driver still with 5 PM shadow and the Mercedes were waiting at the curb.

"I drove down to Vassar last night and stayed with an old girlfriend," the driver said as we moved toward the river. "She says you're right. I've got some student loan money left over and I'm going to buy a cab. The hell with archeology."

"Smart girl. Hang on to her."

"That probably won't work. She says she is going into investment banking. I don't need to live with that."

Once on the River Road we drove by woods and overgrown pasture and several gatehouses leading into estates. Then in a particularly wooded area we came to an open rusted gate and a mottled sign that said "Randolph Park. Keep Out." Behind the gate was a Gothic stone gatehouse.

"I think we're here," the driver said, drove through the gateway and parked. As soon as I emerged from the back seat, the door of the gatehouse opened and a tall man in a worn blue blazer stepped out. Two large brown hounds behind him emitted low snarls.

"Mr. Hume, I presume?" the man said pleasantly through his closed teeth. "Do come in."

I bowed my head.

"Your Royal Highness," I said.

About the Author

James Baar is a writer, blogger, international corporate communications consultant, former business executive and Washington journalist and sometime college lecturer. His latest books: *Conversations at the Redwood: The Portraits Speak*, an historical novel in which some 60 of the historic dead talk again; *Trump Card: Holding America's Enemies at Bay* tells the inside story of the birth of nuclear deterrence; *The Real Thing and other Tales*, a collection of short fiction; But *Wait! There's More! (maybe)*, coauthored with Donald E. Creamer, dissects chaos in the $500 billion global ad business. Baar is also author of two satirical business novels, *Ultimate Severance*, a spin–soaked excursion through an Enroned world featuring designer murder, and *The Great Free Enterprise Gambit*, an instructive story of a highly hostile mega–business takeover and related messy public affairs; also *Spinspeak II: The Dictionary of Language Pollution*; and more than 50 short stories. He lives in Providence, RI, with his wife, Beverly.